The Spring Miracle

K Alice Thompson

A SPRING MIRACLE

ISBN: 9798838880444

Dedication

This book is dedicated to Lilyrose, my dearest friend, for helping

me feel confident in my ability to read and write, and supporting

me in my learning journey. I couldn't have done this without you!

Part One: The Panic

It was a cold misty day. The wind sent cold shivers down each person's spine. It was dark! There was an abundant amount of decaying, fallen branches that covered the mountain forest. Brown moss coated the trees. Ice stood on the edge of each of the trees like razor sharp knives. The icicles were hanging from the trees; they were as cold as an igloo in the Antarctic. When the

water drizzled down the icicle, it made a

lovely tune, like an orchestra playing

classical music when it hit onto the tree

branches. The clouds coated the mountain

like the water of a river.

Above the forest, which was as dark as the

midnight sky, the sun was beaming like a

child smiling. There were sections of the mountain trees that were not decaying at all. The mountains were highly risen above the rocky ground. Plastered with ice cold snow, the mountain tips sat in the sky.

A deep booming noise erupted, and the bottom of the mountain became a cascade of white. The mist grabbed at the bottom of the mountain. Within the terrific mountains, a person stood playing with something. There was an animal sitting beside them. It looked like the animal responded to the noise of a whistle, and it began to run. It was a girl with her dog. The young, brave, and adventurous girl with brown hair was happily playing with her dog. She was full of joy when she was with her amazing dog.

Elegantly, her dark, brown, and curly hair swung in the wind. A red cape perched on her shoulders, keeping her warm from the crisp wind. Her name was Ruby.

Her dog's name was Midnight; this was because of his jet-black fur. His ember eyes poked out of his soft, inky fur. He had an innocent look on his face, and his tail had a

continuous wag.

With a firm grasp, Ruby was holding a

wooden stick with her small hand. It

resembled an old person's cane. It towered

over her. Three quarters of the way up the

stick, a leaf hung from the cane. The

mahogany brown wood was twisted into a

strong cane, as strong as an iron tower.

She walked towards the horizon until they

came to a cloudy area around them. She was

terrified and apprehensive, but she

continued to walk into the mist.

Midnight squatted next to her as she continued walking down. She felt the uneven rocks under her feet. It led them down to a creepy part of the mountain. Clouds trapped them within the darkness.

There was a tree, an extremely spooky tree, that had a nest containing small white eggs. Even though there were no birds in sight, the eggs were cracked into a million pieces.

The branches looked like fingers moving

slowly in the wind. Plants were covered in

moss that looked like frozen snow. Vines

were latched onto the upcoming rocks. The

adventurous girl trudged her way through

the dark place, feeling increasingly more

comfortable. She was feeling anxious, yet eager, to see what caused the thundering clouds. Was it a storm coming, or was it something worse? The questions rushed through her head. There was skittering of creatures under the crinkling floor. She looked up and around, the forest was coated with petrifying vines. They were latched onto every tree in sight. Birds fluttered above the darkness, tree roots had erupted from the ground, the wind grew colder and icicles grew longer. Gazing upwards, the sun was blocked by the pitch-black clouds. The lighting got dimmer and dimmer.

Ruby gazed at an ugly and hideous object that seemed to live there. She wondered what it could be. She was surrounded by dead plants. Ruby wondered what had happened; she visited this place every day with Midnight, and it never looked anything like this before. Could it have been a mystical creature that had turned the world dark? Was it someone who was full of misery?

Ruby headed in to discover more of what she could see. She heard a crack under the floor, so rushed to find Midnight. Ruby stuttered, "It seems haunted here. Something bad could happen. We should leave! At least until the sunlight returns."

Ruby produced an important plan, but suddenly Midnight started to bark loudly, spinning around and around in fast paced circles. Ruby muttered to Midnight, "I will keep you safe, stay with me. I promise!"

Wind started to move more rapidly. Ruby stared at the sky as it started to shift mysteriously. Confused, her eyes darted towards Midnight. She had to keep him safe!

Rocks began to fall again, this time much quicker. Midnight trembled. Barking noises echoed, it happened repeatedly.

Glaring upwards, Ruby still felt nervous and

anxious, slowly feeling horrified by the

thoughts of what could happen. Her head

was filled with questionable ideas. The trees

became more gargantuan. Echoes of

mumbles rippled around her. "R-U-B-Y",

something whispered. She shuddered.

Trees shifted, looking like towering soldiers.

They pushed an icy cold breeze towards her.

Frost came upon her, like something out of a

Disney movie. Her cheeks became swollen

and red. Her face became as pale as a ghost.

She tried to keep warm. She puffed her

warm air into her tiny hands. Ruby latched

onto a stick in the ground and threw it for

Midnight to catch, just as a dog with a bone.

The moss grew to the same length as Midnight's legs. It looked like it was attached to his fur. There were leaves covering the ground like an enormous blanket. It began to cover him, like a woollen blanket at home.

He galloped into the darkness with no one with him. It was him alone. No one to hear him pant or whimper. Midnight was terrified alone, with trees caging him in. He barked frantically, demanding help from someone, anyone. The miniature dog ran towards a towering rock, it replicated the shape of the Sorting Hat. It was pointed at the top and wide at the bottom. Midnight paused and stared at the horrific rock. It was placed on the edge of vine covered rocks, glued to the ground. Approaching it, the girl followed behind him.

Ruby was feeling jittery and a little dejected. The rock was much taller than her. Midnight was tugging really hard at the roots of the tree, and they began to shift, side to side. Ruby saw him pulling vigorously at the branches. She got closer. Midnight growled angrily at the rock, it glistened and shone like an ancient jewel.

The rock looked like an ancient and corroded fossil covered in tribal markings. It looked like it had been perched there for years and years. 'But it wasn't there yesterday,'she thought to herself. Ruby saw what looked like human outlines carved into the rock. Her footprints left a trail heading

towards the rock.

Part Two: Movement in the Forest

Ruby pointed her wooden cane directed at

the fossilised rock, which was sitting there.

She then sighed and she rubbed her hands

once more. Shockingly, the rock began to

shuffle and rumbled above the ground.

Critters began to run beneath the leaves,

they ran like a stampede. She changed

position of her wooden cane and lunged

towards the magnificent rock.

She smacked the cane against the

ginormous rock, and the whole earth

beneath her feet rumbled. It was like a

volcano had erupted. Wind smashed against

the rock and something powerful hit Ruby's

face. North winds blew and lightning strikes

emblazoned the sky. Ruby shuffled

backwards in fear of what might happen

next. She was terrified already, and the wind

continued to get worse.

She placed her stick sternly on the ground.

Anxiously, she inspected the sky to see what

might have changed. It was still dark and

gloomy. Her mind flurried with ideas, not

incredibly good ones. The trees seemed to have gotten closer together. They had moved, and not by a few centimetres, but by inches. She stepped back and tripped on the overgrown vines and roots of the monstrous trees.

But she did not let that stop her, she leapt to her feet and felt very apprehensive. She was horrified to see rocks tumbling down behind

her. They shifted quicker by the second and

she was panicking, 'What if they land on me

or Midnight?'

The tree branches lifted into the air like a rocket into the atmosphere. It had claws like a dragon that rose from the hard ground. It rumbled like the sound of a herd of elephants. Ruby was in shock that it moved so rapidly. "Trees moving," she thought quietly to herself. The trees continued to move, and the ground shuddered like an earthquake.

The tree branches fell to the ground like a tree struck by thunder and lightning. Ruby glared up at the sky, there was something enormous standing there. It had lights reflecting in its shiny scales. They reflected as fireworks do in the pitch-black sky.

They released a smoke-like material as they

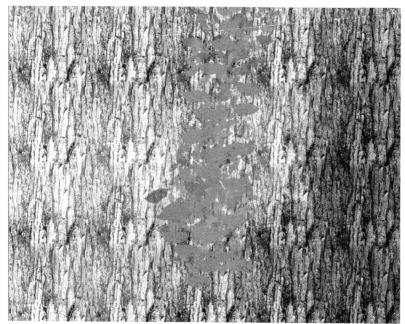

moved. Clouds hung above them like some

sort of storm was about to emerge. The sky

released a radiant blue light that made Ruby

blink. She was nervous again. Clouds of ash

started to get lower to the ground. The

creature was without a face as the clouds

covered him like a cage. The creature

extended its gigantic legs and spread them

around Ruby, trapping her in with no escape.

There was a beak attached to its face, but it

was not a bird. It had enormous legs but

wasn't a giraffe. It was something rare and

extraordinary. Something not found by the best of scientists.

The creature or thing was coming towards her. She launched herself back but was amazed to see such an unordinary thing within the forest she knew well. As it got closer, her wooden cane hit the site of the creature and there was a marvellous tune that echoed from it. It was as if the waves of the sea had joined them in the forest. She crept down onto one knee and again it hit the cane elegantly. It made exotic music that rattled in her ears.

The creature began to bow to Ruby. Its head came in line with Ruby's, and she turned to check on Midnight. Midnight was stunned

into silence by what had happened to him.

It had a meter long set of antennas that

swayed in the wind; they resembled bones

from dinosaurs. Her face began to glisten

and glow. She wasn't scared anymore. She

jumped to her feet and began to stroke her

cane against the side of the creature. She

had a great grin on her face that went from ear to ear. It made the sound of a piano in a cathedral. The mellow tune reverberated throughout the trees, hitting every single branch that it could.

The creature opened its glaring eyes and stared directly at Ruby. It threw itself forward and put his antenna into Ruby's hand. She grasped on tightly and the

creature released a bone of his magical

antenna into her hand. She placed the

luminescent coloured bone into her cane -

she had always wondered why the whole

was placed centralised at the top.

The cane belonged to her great-great grandfather; did he know about the creature? Did he know this would happen?

As soon as it entered the hole, it shone an ember glow.

Part Three: Ember

The wooden cane shone on the top of the stick. It covered over it like fire and ash expelled from an active volcano. Ruby had a grin on her face, like a child who stole sweets from the candy store. Then a variety of plants started to blossom on the top of it. Suddenly, she slammed it down onto the ground like a meteorite that crashed down onto the earth. It made the creature move

by standing up into the air. The creature

looked like it had spikes like a hedgehog.

There was grey smoke that covered the

earth from the top to the bottom of the

ground. Some of the ash was red and grey.

There were lights that were glistening on

the back of the creature. It looked so bright

that someone could see it from a mile away.

The reflection would have hit the other side of the mountain region. It looked like there were two creatures. It looked like a precious family of two or a baby creature with its mother.

The creatures flashed with an illumination of lights that shone on their scaly, lizard-like skin. Suddenly, the trees started to move towards her. Footsteps were coming from a

mile away. She swung her wooden cane

around in the air. The trees were walking

like a herd of elephants that were stomping

around at the zoo.

The trees were crashing into each other, like

cars crashing on the motorway. It came

down really hard towards her. She was

shocked to see it close to her. As the tree landed with a crash onto the ground, she fell to the forest floor with a loud thump. She was stunned at all these weird occurrences. When she fell and had the tree near her body, the wooden cane fell elegantly to the ground. Then the glowing substance fell out of the wooden cane and made a bouncing noise. The gem hit the floor after knocking

on the rocky ground.

Suddenly, the glowing gem carried on rolling down the dark forest floor, making the creature really angry. Then it started to move rapidly across the dark area. The creature opened his enormous mouth when it saw the shining object. Meanwhile, the trees were still walking around behind the creatures. Ruby saw Midnight next to the tree, then she ran with all her speed towards

Midnight, who she was hoping to save. He was in front of the moving trees, and he sprinted towards the beaming gem that was in front of him, like a dog chasing a bone.

The trees with big clumpy feet started coming up behind him with horrific speed. They were chasing Ruby; she was horrified when the trees approached her from behind.

Ruby was panting with all her might, while getting chased by mythical-looking creatures and living trees that had feet like birds and three claws that were as sharp as a vulture. Would the trees, creatures or monster try and capture her? Then Midnight ran towards the object and caught the gem in his mouth. Midnight slammed into the rock with a sad look on his face, he was full

of misery.

Then Ruby ran fast towards Midnight, so the

creature was distracted by the sound of

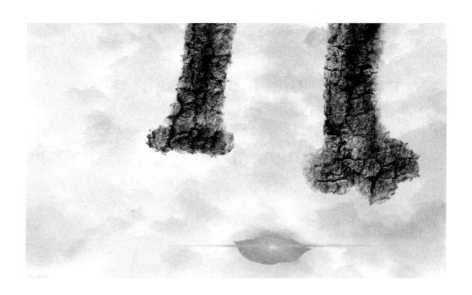

rustling leaves around her, but the trees

walked in front of her before she could get

past them. Then the tree with feet was

above her head, but she ran towards the

gem anyway without being scared. One of

the branches broke into a million pieces. A

weird look crossed Ruby's face as she placed

her wooden cane onto the grey and old

looking ground. She looked up and saw the

tree extremely close to her head. She led her

wooden cane toward the tree's feet. Using

her wooden cane in the air like magic, she

decided to lay it on the floor gently. Then

she gazed at her wooden cane when it began

to glow again, and she thought it was just

like a magic wand, like Dumbledore uses in

the Harry Potter movies.

Part Four: Peace in Spring

She realised that, with this cane, she could

control the movement of the creatures. She

was trying to decide what to do with this

tree with bird feet that were perched above

her head. She lifted her cane and made the

tree swing through the air when she moved

her stick towards the tree creature, and

then positioned the cane in such a way that

the tree's foot elegantly landed on the floor, elegantly. She looked at the cane with suspicion then she said, "oh," when she looked at the ground where the gem landed before. Then she had a look around and saw Midnight biting at the rock (again). He began to bark loudly, then he shook his head at Ruby with a humongous smile. Ruby smiled back at him with glee.

She wondered, "What should I do with the

creatures now?" She looked up into the sky

then looked back down at Midnight, and

then she slammed the cane down to the ground. Suddenly, she made the creature start to move away from herself. Then the area with rocks, which coated the floor, was also covered with grey ash and there was a mountain in the distance between the layers of grass and ash. The rock looked like sedimentary rocks layered over thousands of years. Then the ash moved like fire in the distance. Ruby appeared from the middle of the grey smoky ash.

Ruby strolled backwards with her cane lit up (she had a grin on her face). The creature's smoke looked like candy floss in a sweet shop when it was perched there in the distance. From the mountain, Ruby caught a glimpse of a light beaming on them. She could see their legs clearly now. Each

creature had four human-like legs with

claws. They were walking toward Ruby and

Midnight. Then they shifted like clouds in

the daylight sky.

Appearing behind the clouds, the sun shone,

creating a horizon. Trees hung around with

leaves blossoming from their cold core. Then

the stalactites started to melt away when the sun appeared in the sky. They dripped with water. There was a grey and rocky ground with igneous rocks beneath the clouds. They were scattered across the ground.

Suddenly, the ground, which was once grey, now magically turned green. Grass started to shoot out around them, covering the

ground like a blanket. The flowers started

blossoming with an array of multicoloured

plants with all shapes and sizes. The rock

was still there with moss growing around it,

but it was not dark anymore. There were

birds tweeting around the area that had

trees. There were birds flying around in the

air in the distance, and there was a

mountain protruding from the ground. Ruby and Midnight were standing at the edge of the horizon and Midnight was sitting on the rock. He watched as Ruby pulled the shiny object from her wooden cane and started to trek towards the rocky hills that look like a waterfall.

Ruby attached the shiny object to the chain that was hanging there. It was covered with several other objects from many creatures. This could not have been the first sighting of them. Ruby was happy, then Midnight jumped onto Ruby's chest and started licking her face. As Ruby stepped back and stared into the sky, she realised there were millions of objects from creatures. It must have been from generations and even her

great grandfather's generation, as he gave

her the cane in the first instance.

The End

Acknowledgments

Amy Elizabeth (Founder of the Positivity Pack) and the people in Mind Freedom for helping me to design the perfect front cover.

Printed in Great Britain
by Amazon

83305969R00041